INTO THE BUCKET

Illustrated by Art Mawhinney

Random House 🏠 **New York**

A Random House PICTUREBACK® Book

Copyright © 2006 CCI Entertainment Ltd.
HARRY AND HIS BUCKET FULL OF DINOSAURS and all related characters
and elements are trademarks of and © CCI Entertainment Ltd. All rights reserved.
Published in the United States by Random House Children's Books,
a division of Random House, Inc., New York.

PICTUREBACK, RANDOM HOUSE and colophon, and PLEASE READ TO ME
and colophon are registered trademarks of Random House, Inc.

www.randomhouse.com/kids

Library of Congress Control Number: 2006922096

ISBN-13: 978-0-375-83867-5

ISBN-10: 0-375-83867-8

Printed in the United States of America   10 9 8 7 6 5 4 3 2 1   First Edition

"Harry, we have to go," Mom called. "We don't want to
be late to pick up Nana."

Harry was under the bed. "I'm coming," Harry called
back. "I want to wear the cap Nana gave me, but I can't
find it."

"Where can it be?" Harry asked his dinosaurs. "I just had it this morning."

"Is it orange?" asked Taury.

"Yes!" said Harry.

"With a brown brim? And a yellow *H* on the front?" asked Taury.

"That's it!" cried Harry. "Where is it?"

"Haven't seen it," Taury teased.

"I've *got* to find it," Harry said. "I want to wear it when we pick up Nana."

Patsy looked on top of the dresser. No cap.

Taury looked under the art table. No cap.

Harry looked in the closet. No cap.

"We've just *got* to find it!" said Harry.

Harry heard Sid ask, "What is everyone looking for?"

"My cap," answered Harry. "We can't find it anywhere."

"Hmmm," Sid said. "I just saw Trike with it."

"Where was he?" asked Harry. He looked for Sid. "Hey, Sid, where are *you*?"

"In Dino-World," said Sid. His voice was coming from *inside the bucket!*

"Where?"

"You know, Dino-World . . . ," said Sid's voice again, ". . . in the bucket."

Harry looked over at the bucket. There was a faint glow coming out of it.

The glow was getting brighter.

Harry looked at the dinosaurs. Just then a couple of small stars shot up out of the bucket.

"Wow!" shouted Harry. "I thought the bucket was empty."

"Not really, Harry," Taury answered. "You should give it another look."

Suddenly Pterence flew up out of the bucket. "Come on, Harry, let's go!" he said. "You're going to love Dino-World!" Pterence turned around and flew right back into the bucket.

"What's it like there, Pterence?" called Harry.

"It's called Dino-World, isn't it?" laughed Taury. "Imagine how fun and exciting it's going to be. And the only way to get there is to jump!"

"Let's go! . . . On three!" And they counted together.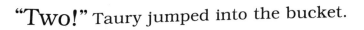

"One!" Patsy jumped into the bucket.

"Two!" Taury jumped into the bucket.

"Three!" And Harry jumped into the bucket.

"You made it, Harry!" cheered Patsy.
"I knew you'd find it," said Taury.
"When you needed to," added Sid.

"Wow!" said Harry. "This is the coolest place ever."

"It's more fun than a frog on a Ferris wheel," said Patsy.

"It's even *better* than that!" said Steggy.

"But it's so big!" marveled Harry. "How are we ever going to find Trike and my cap?"

"There are lots of places to look, so let's go," said Taury.

They went to Pepper Rock and there was a *neat* cave.

But no Trike.
And no cap.

They went to the edge of the Primordial Swamp and
called Trike's name. There was *lots* of mud.

But no Trike.
And no cap.

Then they went to Rock Lake. The water was blue and cool.

But no Trike.
And no cap.

"Sometimes Trike climbs Pillow Hill. The top is soft and bouncy," Sid explained to Harry. "And even if he isn't there, it's high enough that we might see him."

But when they got there, Trike wasn't at the top of Pillow Hill. In fact, he was nowhere in sight.

"We're *never* going to find Trike and my cap," sighed Harry. "Dino-World is just too big!"

"Hey, I have an idea," said Pterence excitedly. He pointed at a little clump of bushes in the distance. "What if we go to the Wishing Well and wish that we could find Trike and the cap?"

"Great plan, Pterence," said Taury. And they all hurried off.

Soon they were standing beside the Wishing Well.

Harry closed his eyes and began to wish. "I—" Just then Trike walked out of the bushes! He was wearing Harry's cap . . . *on his nose horn!*

"Trike!" cried all the dinosaurs.

"My cap!" cried Harry.

"Aw, Harry," said Trike. "I thought it was a cap for me . . . it matches my colors just right."

"Sorry, Trike," said Harry. "Nana gave it to me. I really want to stay and explore Dino-World, but I have to go!"

"That's okay, Harry," said Taury. "There will always be time for Dino-World later."

"Mom, I'm coming! I found my cap!"

Harry, Sam, and Mom picked Nana up at the store. Harry was excited to tell her all about Dino-World. He told her about jumping in the bucket. He told her about the Primordial Swamp. He told her about the cave at Pepper Rock. He told her about all of the things he could see from high up on Pillow Hill.

"Oh, Harry," said Nana. "That is so exciting. Did you
make a wish at the Wishing Well?"

"No, I didn't have time . . . ," Harry began. And then he stopped.

"Wait a minute, Nana. I didn't even tell you about the Wishing Well yet. . . ."

Harry looked at Nana. She was looking out the car window and smiling. Harry wondered, *How does Nana know about the Wishing Well in Dino-World???*